GEOFFREY S

D0508835

Jill Murphy wrote the first draft of *Geoffrey Strangeways* when she was fourteen; it came second in the school literary competition. One of the reasons it's taken her so long to finish, she says, is that "I wrote it first without pictures and full of horses – and I can't draw horses, so I had to use lots of reference material!"
In the meantime, she wrote and illustrated lots of very popular children's books, including three about the Worst Witch and three about the elephant Large family – *Five Minutes' Peace* (winner of the Best Book for Babies Award), *All in One Piece* and *A Piece of Cake* – as well as a novel for older readers, *Worlds Apart*. She has also recently produced a small son.

Books by the same author

A Bad Spell for the Worst Witch
The Worst Witch
The Worst Witch Strikes Again
Worlds Apart

Picture books

All in One Piece
Five Minutes' Peace
On the Way Home
Peace at Last
A Piece of Cake
Whatever Next!

GEOFFREY STRANGEWAYS

Written and illustrated by
JILL MURPHY

WALKER BOOKS
LONDON

TO MAC

WITH LOVE FOREVER

First published 1990 by Walker Books Ltd
87 Vauxhall Walk, London SE11 5HJ

© 1990 Jill Murphy

This edition published 1991
Reprinted 1991

Printed and bound in Great Britain by
Richard Clay Ltd, Bungay, Suffolk

British Library Cataloguing in Publication Data
Murphy, Jill
Geoffrey Strangeways.
I. Title
823'.914 [J]
ISBN 0-7445-1722-2

CONTENTS

Chapter One

 eoffrey did not want to go home. For this reason he was dawdling along as slowly as possible without actually stopping altogether. In the end, even this idle pace seemed to be propelling him too hastily in the direction of his village, so he shuffled to a halt and looked for somewhere to sit down.

The country lane was flanked by steep, grassy banks, with gnarled trees and weathered bushes growing all along the top. Halfway down the bank, one of these trees had rooted itself horizontally, just asking to be sat upon, so Geoffrey nipped up and wedged himself among the branches like a stork settling into its nest.

It was late afternoon on a baking hot day in June, and there was no wind to blow away the stale air wafting up in waves from the cracked earth road. Geoffrey was exhausted, having spent the entire day walking ten miles to the nearest market town of Axington, trying to find work and walking all the way back again. He was only eleven years old, but in those days you tried to find work as soon as it was necessary, and in Geoffrey's case it was extremely necessary.

The trouble was that he was fussy. He did not want to end up as a dishwasher in some dreadful, greasy tavern kitchen, being bellowed at by a great, fat cook while the sun blazed away outside. He didn't want to spend seven days a week bent double in the fields for a few pence a day.

In fact, the only thing that Geoffrey wanted in the whole world was to be a knight, and he knew that there was absolutely no chance of this happening except in his dreams, and dreams were not good enough.

Everything was against Geoffrey in his

ambition to become Sir Geoffrey Strangeways, or Sir Geoffrey of the Crimson Gauntlets as he sometimes imagined. For a start, he was extremely poor. He lived alone with his widowed mother, who fortunately was very good at knitting and managed to sell enough vests, stockings and the like to keep them from starving. (Big jumpers and knitted outer-garments had not caught on in the Middle Ages, or she could have made a lot more money.) As it was, she was a very speedy knitter, and could turn out three pairs of knitted hose (a garment rather like modern tights), two medium-sized vests, and one balaclava to be worn underneath a knight's helmet, all in the space of two days.

However, only last week she had fallen off the back of her brother Harold's ox-cart on her way home from the village Summer Hop (and here it must be confessed that she had consumed a fraction too much mead and was unsteady on her feet at the time), and had broken not just one but both arms, which were now all done up in splints and would take ages to mend. In this way, the burden of earning their living had suddenly descended like a lead-lined winter coat on to Geoffrey's frail shoulders; and frail shoulders they were indeed.

Not only was Geoffrey poor – and everyone knew that you had to be a lord's son or else do something madly brave in battle before you could even be considered as a trainee knight – but he was also a small and rather scruffy-looking person. His clothing was either miles too large because of growing-room, or miles too small because he had grown out of them. Either way, he always managed to look absolutely dreadful, and his dark hair, sprouting in clumps of wild curls like an overgrown shrub, did not improve the picture. He also had one front tooth missing where he had stepped on a rake and it had leapt upright and bashed him in the face. In fact he was unbelievably clumsy, driving his mother to distraction by dropping all her precious plates, accidentally tearing curtains from the wall, and even treading on balls of wool and yanking all the stitches from her ever-clicking knitting needles. All things considered, Geoffrey was not the sort of person who would instantly have spring to mind as a likely candidate for knighthood.

Geoffrey sat glumly in the tree with his bird-like legs dangling over the edge, thinking about the awful day that lay behind him.

At Axington he had tried half-heartedly for two jobs that his mother had pointed out in the local news-sheet. One was in a candlemaker's and the other was in a bakery. To tell the truth, he hadn't exactly *tried* for either of them. "Now then, lad," asked the manager of the bakery. "What makes you feel that you are the right young man to come and work for me?"

"*I* don't know," Geoffrey had replied, hands in pockets, trying to look as gormless as possible. "I s'pose I couldn't think of anything else to do or something." He had done the same at the candlemaker's, and as there were at least fifteen youngsters applying for each position, all doing their best to look bright and hard-working, Geoffrey was not considered for one moment as a suitable applicant, much to his relief at the time.

However, sitting in the tree, with his home village lurking round the next bend in the lane, he suddenly felt guilty, thinking of his poor injured mum waiting hopefully for her son to return with some good news – and he also felt hungry, for their food supplies were getting low and he had eaten only a boiled egg and a lettuce sandwich during the whole day, which had begun at dawn.

The shadows lengthened and the birds began to sing in that extra-loud way which they do in the early and late hours of the day. Geoffrey glanced up at the scarlet sun, large and flat as if someone had cut it out of paper and pasted it on to the sky, and knew there was no more avoiding it. He would have to walk the last few yards and see his mother's face fall with disappointment when he told her that he didn't have a job. "I did try, Mother," he would say, looking at the floor. "But they didn't want me."

Well, it wasn't *exactly* a lie. He had tried inasmuch as he had walked twenty miles there and back for the interviews.

As he clambered out of the tree, accidently catching his threadbare sleeve on a branch and ripping it clean off the rest of his best interview shirt, he heard the sound of a horse and rider approaching. The whole of the lane, from the trees to the earth floor, began to vibrate as the rhythmic thudding of hoofs drew nearer, and Geoffrey could scarcely believe his luck when a knight, clad in full armour, on an enormous white charger, came thundering up the road and reined to a halt next to him.

Chapter Two

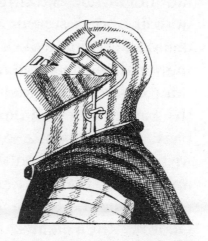

"ood evening, lad," boomed an unearthly voice through the closed visor. "Can you tell me, is this next village named Over-Wallop-on-the-Hill?"

Geoffrey stood frozen with awe, half in and half out of the tree, his back towards the road and his head turned almost a hundred and eighty degrees like an owl. Words completely failed him as he gazed at the shining, silver helmet and the cloak, which was made of brilliant green velvet with a huge golden rampant lion embroidered on the back. Chainmail was visible at the joints of the shining armour, and the wonderful white horse had obviously ridden fast and far, judging by the condition of its flaring nostrils and glistening coat; not that you could see very much of the creature, for it was wearing a coat and face protector of the same design as its rider's cloak. Tied on to the back of the saddle was a profusion of bags and weapons, a sort of clipboard with writing on it and a small wicker basket which appeared to contain a pigeon.

The knight pushed back his visor, and Geoffrey saw a clean-shaven, sunburnt face of about forty years old, with a long aristocratic nose and very blue eyes surrounded by laugh lines.

"CAN–YOU–NOT–HEAR, BOY?" asked the knight very loudly and slowly, thinking that Geoffrey must be the village idiot.

Geoffrey snapped out of his trance. "Oh yes, s-s-sir," he burbled, forgetting that he was still in the tree, taking a step backwards and plummeting several feet on to the road. The horse shifted from one foot to the other, and Geoffrey jumped up and dusted himself down. His sleeve was still in the tree and he felt rather ridiculous with one skinny, white arm sticking out of the mutilated shirt.

The knight's eyes crinkled in amusement. He was used to small boys, and even grown men, going all weak at the knees at the sight of him. Being a knight in those days was a bit like being a famous actor nowadays; everyone wanted to become a knight because it looked such a glamorous occupation.

The knight looked down at the little boy, who was blushing from head to toe in his curious one-armed shirt, and felt a wave of sympathy towards him. "The next village, lad," he repeated. "Is it Over-Wallop-on-the-Hill?"

"No, s-sir," replied Geoffrey in a voice which sounded even squeakier than usual. "The next village is Under-Withy-on-the-Marsh. It's my own village, sir, so I know which one it is. Over-Wallop is ten miles from my village. You go straight through and keep north through Little Rollaround and Great Rollaround, and you're there."

"Are you hungry, lad?" asked the knight, quite suddenly.

"I'm always hungry, sir," Geoffrey admitted with a smirk. He always smirked, his lips pressed together to hide the gappy front teeth.

"Then join me for supper," said the knight, and to Geoffrey's utter amazement this fabulous person tethered his horse to the same tree which Geoffrey had just fallen out of, and began rummaging in one of the saddle-bags. Geoffrey almost drooled with anticipation as the knight brought out a flask and several bulging paper bags.

"Hold these a second, would you?" said the knight, shoving everything into Geoffrey's arms as he fiddled with some buckles and removed the gleaming helmet.

"That's better," he commented, easing his cramped neck by moving it from side to side, and running a hand through his hair which was straight and black, and rather slicked down from being pressed beneath the heavy helmet. "It's really not the day to be wearing this sort of stuff. I feel like a chicken being baked in an oven and it takes about ten years to get it all off, so I'm stuck in it till bedtime. Why don't you hop back into your tree and use your lap as a table? I'll lean against the bank here. The tree wouldn't last five seconds if I sat on it in this lot. Here, use this old bit of rag as a tablecloth."

The old bit of rag was Geoffrey's sleeve

which the knight had taken from the branch and handed to him. Geoffrey's blush deepened.

"If you please, sir," he said, feeling as wriggly as a caterpillar, "it isn't exactly a piece of rag, it's my sleeve sir, and I have to take it home and sew it on or I'll be in the most awful trouble."

The knight burst out laughing, then hastily composed his face into a serious expression, for he was exceptionally courteous and considerate (as most knights are, in fact), and realized that he had hurt the boy's feelings by referring to part of his clothing as an old rag.

"Please forgive me," said the knight. "My eyesight is not as good as it used to be. If I had looked more carefully I would have *noticed* that it was part of your shirt. It was only that one does not expect to see a sleeve hanging in a tree, and though I *had* noticed that your shirt had only one arm, I must confess that I thought it must be part of some new fashion you youngsters are wearing nowadays. Am I forgiven?"

"Of course, sir," said Geoffrey, nearly fainting with pride that a knight should be asking him for forgiveness.

"Right then!" said the knight, with a dazzling smile. "Up you jump and let's eat. I must be away before long."

Geoffrey bundled the sleeve into his pocket and clambered up the bank, stroking the white charger's soft, whiskery nose as he passed it by. The paper bags contained an entire chicken neatly cut into pieces, several baked lamb chops, a dozen cold roast potatoes, a whole loaf neatly buttered and fitted back together again, tied lengthways with a piece of string to stop the butter getting all over the place, two chocolate éclairs, with cream which *had* got all over the place, and a large bag of nuts and raisins. The flask was full of Earl Grey tea. Geoffrey nearly wept for joy at the sight of it all. He and his mother could live on this supper for a week.

As if reading his mind, the knight suddenly said, "Do you have any relatives at home?"

"Only my mother," answered Geoffrey.

"Then let's make up a little picnic for you to take home to her, shall we?" said the knight, stuffing two chops, several slices of bread and one of the somewhat mangled éclairs into a bag. "Now, let's get on with it!"

The knight, who was the very model of

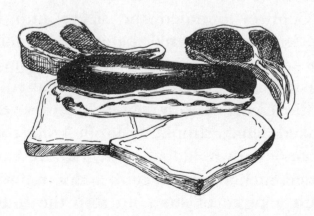

chivalry, knew that Geoffrey would be too embarrassed to help himself, so he made a neat pile of bits and pieces on a paper bag as a plate and handed it to him. "That's for you," he announced firmly.

"Thank you, sir," gasped Geoffrey.

For a while there was no sound except for the birds still shrilling and singing goodnight to the world, the rustling and clanking of the charger as he shifted about restlessly, and the steady munching of two very hungry people.

"Why are you going to Over-Wallop, sir?" asked Geoffrey, through a mouthful of roast potato. (Manners were not Geoffrey's strong point.)

"I'm on an assignment," said the knight.

"Hic! What's that?" asked Geoffrey, who was eating so fast that he had given himself an attack of the hiccups.

"It's when you're given a job to do," explained the knight. "And then, well – you go off and do it. Actually, I've got three assignments and they're all in this county, so I'm going to do them one after the other!"

"Who gives you – hic! – the assignments?" asked Geoffrey.

"Well," said the knight, "I work for a big agency in Axington. It's called 'Freelance Rescue Services Limited' in Old Barrow Street. I expect there's an advert for it in that news-sheet of yours. Give it here a moment. Have you heard of us?"

Geoffrey handed over the news-sheet, and the knight began to look through it.

"Of *course* I've heard of you, sir," replied Geoffrey, even more impressed than ever. "The whole *country*'s heard of Freelance Rescue Services!"

"Here we are," said the knight. He folded back the news-sheet and read aloud:

"PROBLEMS?
Then bring them to us at:
FREELANCE RESCUE SERVICES LTD
Specialists in any distressing situation.
Established 125 years.
Dragons despatched.
Damsels rescued from villainous uncles/
wicked stepmothers/fiendish fathers.
Villages liberated from tyrants/ogres/
giants etc.
Any evil-doer taken on.
Reasonable terms.

*Weekly payments in cases of genuine
hardship.
Team of expert knights at our disposal.
Slightly higher rate for the famous
Sir Walter of Winterwood.
No commission too small.*

*MOTTO:
NEVER TURN BACK BEFORE
THE DEED IS DONE*

*Come to us at 12 Old Barrow Street, Axington,
or we have a large stock of
carrier-pigeons at our disposal."*

"Gosh!" said Geoffrey. "It must be wonderful to be one of the Freelance knights. I wish *I* was."

"It's not all *that* wonderful, to tell you the honest truth," said the knight, pouring out a beakerful of tea and handing it to Geoffrey. "It's very exhausting work. Would you like to hear my schedule?"

"Yes, please!" nodded Geoffrey, delighted to be spoken to as if he was a fellow knight sharing a tea-break.

The knight detached the clipboard from the saddle and looked at the list. "Job number one," he read. "Ah yes. Damsel in deep distress locked in small tower south of Over-Wallop-on-the-Hill near Falcon's Perch (clump of pine trees on ridge). Wicked uncle (guardian of damsel) camping in hut below."

"Crumbs!" said Geoffrey. "What will you do to the uncle? Will you run him through? How will you get her out? Will you have to get a ladder?"

"Well, for a start," said the knight, "there's usually a staircase inside a tower. I expect the uncle will have the key. It's only very occasionally that someone is shut up in a tower with no way in except the window. In fact, I only know of one case – Rapunzel she was called, dreadful business that. It isn't always a tower either, sometimes it's a shed, or an attic of an ordinary cottage. Anyway, it rarely comes to violence with any of the captors. The sight of a knight with his sword at the ready is usually enough to frighten them out of their wits, and the whole thing is often settled over a cup of tea. Have you finished your tea by the way? There's only one beaker and I quite fancy a cup myself."

"Would you like to finish mine for me?" said Geoffrey, who had been sipping it with his nose wrinkled up. He was only used to straightforward kitchen-teapot-type tea, and had never had anything fancy like Earl Grey. "It tastes a bit like perfume, doesn't it?"

"Lovely stuff," said the knight, knocking it back in one gulp. "Where was I? Oh yes, damsels. Actually, my wife was a damsel in a tower when I first met her. Rescued her from her appalling grandfather, Boris the Brute he was called, and quite right too!

How on earth he ever had anything to do with such a perfect creature as my wife I shall never be able to fathom. Anyway, that's all quite beside the point. Job number two. Ah now, this one should be a piece of cake. Dragon's lair in Rottcliff. It's an old one – been empty for years – but there have been reports that fire and smoke have been spotted up there at night, and the villagers think there may be a new pair of the blighters come back to nest. I expect it's just some local lads mucking about having camp-fires and the like. I'll soon sort them out.

"Job number three. Not so easy this one. A very unpleasant ogre, name of Grobb. Evil chap, one bloodshot eye slap bang in the middle of his forehead. Got the whole village of Rowanbank scared to go out of doors even in broad daylight. Might take a week that one, and it might get nasty.

"Anyway, that's what it's all about really, being a knight. Travel, tact and toughness if necessary. My poor wife Elaine gets awfully fed up stuck at home with our two youngsters, worrying about me all the time. Still, at least she understands, having been a distressed damsel herself."

"Who actually asks for your help?" asked Geoffrey. "It can't be the damsels in distress if they are locked up in their towers."

"Ah well," said the knight. "In their case, it's usually a villager who suspects something funny is going on, or the uncle's wife or something like that. But with the ogre, the mayor of the village had a meeting with the council, and they decided to call us in. They pay for us out of the taxes, you know. Same goes for the dragon's lair."

The lane was fast disappearing into shadow and Geoffrey could only make out the shape of the knight in the gloom.

"Well," said the knight, "I really must be off now."

He screwed up all the paper bags and shoved them into the largest one, then put them back into the saddle-bag with the flask.

"Don't forget your news-sheet," he said, picking it up from where it lay in the branches and handing it to Geoffrey. (Knights are very litter-conscious.) "Now then, would you like a lift into the village as I'm going that way?"

This was the crowning moment of

Geoffrey's miraculous evening. The knight helped him up on to the vast charger and they galloped off down the lane, Geoffrey hanging on round the knight's waist for dear life. This is it, he thought to himself. I've just got to be a knight. Nothing else will do, not in the whole world. I've *got* to do it.

 eality loomed as they drew up outside Geoffrey's mother's cottage, a tiny tumble-down affair with tatty grey thatch full of birds and beetles. There was, however, a very nice lavender bush outside the window, and a large brightly lit lantern on a hook, which cast jagged shadows up the path. To Geoffrey's great annoyance, absolutely no one was about in the village street to witness his return home.

"Thank you so much for everything," said Geoffrey, slithering from the saddle.

"A pleasure," said the knight. "Sir Walter of Winterwood at your service. Regards to your mother." And he snapped his visor shut and was off in a flash of hooves into the black street. He was a knight with style.

"Good heavens!" breathed Geoffrey, awestruck. "I just had supper with Sir Walter of Winterwood. *The* Sir Walter of Winterwood!" He remained standing transfixed by the gatepost, quite overcome with a mixture of shock and pure delight.

"Geoffrey?" called his mother's voice from behind the front door. "Is that you?"

Geoffrey shook himself out of his trance and hurried up the short path to the front door.

"Yes, Mum," he replied, pushing it open. "Sorry I'm a bit late."

"A *bit* late!" exclaimed his mother, looking extremely annoyed. "I've been worrying myself *sick* these past hours, and when it got dark – well! That's *it*, I said to myself. He's been set on by a band of cut-throats and I shall be left all alone in the world."

The look on her face suddenly changed from stern to indulgent. "Anyway," she continued. "You're home now, safe and sound." And she attempted to fling her arms around him, which was rather awkward as her arms were encased in heavy wooden splints.

Geoffrey felt extremely sore and bruised by the time she had finished, but he knew how worried she had been, so he bore it bravely.

"Now then," said his mother, sitting down in the rocking-chair by the fire. "Sit yourself down and tell me what you've been up to all this time. I'll make you some dinner in a moment. There are only three eggs left, but there's still half a sack of potatoes. It won't take a minute to make eggy-potatoes for our dinner, will it?"

Geoffrey sat down on the low stool at his mother's feet, and as he did so, she caught sight of his mangled shirt.

"Oh, *Geoffrey*!" she exclaimed. "*Look* at your shirt! And it's your best one. How *could* you be so careless? Now *just* you explain to me where you've been all this time, my lad."

Geoffrey looked at her as she settled back in the rocking-chair and began rocking grimly backwards and forwards, her fingers at the end of the splints looking lost and empty without any knitting in them. The firelight and the two lanterns hanging on either side of the room cast dancing shadows everywhere.

Geoffrey's mother was very small. She was wearing a faded blue dress, a voluminous white apron and a starched white cap with a frill round the front. Her unruly hair, exactly like Geoffrey's only more so, escaped in corkscrews all round the edges. She was only twenty-nine, but looked much older from being overworked and half-starved so much of the time. Her son felt a wave of tenderness sweep over him as he looked at her anxious face.

"I've been having supper with Sir Walter of Winterwood," he announced proudly.

"*Really*, Geoffrey," said his mother. "I'm not a *complete* idiot."

Geoffrey was rather taken aback by this. It hadn't occurred to him that she would not believe him.

"It's *true!*" he squeaked indignantly. "Look here, I can prove it. He gave me some of our supper to bring home for you. Look!"

Geoffrey pulled the paper bag of food from his pocket and gave it to her. The contents were a little squashed, but still looked most appetizing to his mother who had eaten only a boiled egg, a plate of porridge and two raw carrots all day.

"Bless my soul!" she gasped. "Where on earth did all this come from?"

"I already *told* you," replied Geoffrey, feeling exasperated. "It's from Sir Walter of Winterwood. He stopped me in the lane to ask me the way and then he offered me half his supper. Oh Mother, he was so wonderful. Why, he treated me as if I was a knight myself. I wish I was. I'd be so brave, doing all those deeds! I'd — "

"Yes, dear," said his mother fondly. "But did you get either of those jobs we saw in the news-sheet?"

"Well actually, no, I didn't, as a matter of fact," mumbled Geoffrey.

"Oh, *Geoffrey!*" said his mother, in heavy tones. "Whatever will become of us? You know I can't get knitting again for ages yet, and we'll just starve if you don't get something soon. It's all very well spending half the day chatting with Sir Walter Wonderful or whatever his name is but – oh, Geoffrey!" And she began to cry, very quietly, her tears dropping neatly into the paper bag on her lap.

Geoffrey felt so awful that, in a moment of lunacy, he decided to pretend he had found some work after all. "It's all right, Mother!" he exclaimed. "Don't cry any more. I *did* get a job and it's far better than those boring old ones I was hoping for. Sir Walter was so impressed by me that he told me to come along to the agency tomorrow morning and he'd make sure I was taken on."

"Truly?" asked his mother, wiping her eyes with the hem of her apron, a watery smile hovering uncertainly at the corners of her mouth.

"Absolutely truly, cross my heart!" Geoffrey reassured her, the matter now completely out of hand. "He said I'd go far, a young fellow like me, and that the agency would be proud to have me!"

Geoffrey's mother was delighted at this wonderful news, and treated her already battered son to another agonizing hug with the splints. "Well, you'd better get that shirt off and sew the sleeve back on again," she laughed, bustling into action. "I'd do it for you myself, but I can't with my arms like this. Why didn't you tell me all about the job when you came in? But it really is marvellous, isn't it? And such an exciting job, Geoffrey. I am so proud of you. You'd better have an early night if you are to be up again at dawn with a tcn-mile walk ahead of you. What sort of things will they be asking you to do at the agency? Did they tell you?"

"Oh, all sorts of different things," muttered Geoffrey vaguely, pulling off his shirt and reaching for the sewing-box. "They said they'd start me in the office helping with the filing, then they'll let me go to knight-school to learn about sword-fighting and slaying dragons and all that, and then when I've grown a bit they said they'd probably make me a real knight."

"Well I never," said his mum. "Fancy that. And I always thought that you had to be a noble lord's son before they'd even think of you as a knight. Well, it just goes to show how times are changing, doesn't it?"

Geoffrey bent over the needlework to hide his guilty face as his mother prattled happily on. Now he'd *really* done it. He'd just have to set off the next morning and try to persuade them at the agency that they needed yet another office-boy or groom. Even as he thought about it, he knew it was an impossible task. The only chance he stood was if Sir Walter was there, but Sir Walter had said that he might be away for a week. Anyway, he had only shared his food with Geoffrey, nothing had been said about a job.

Lying in bed that night, listening to the night rustlings in the thatch, he found it impossible to sleep, as he imagined coming home the next day and admitting that the whole thing had been a lie. That's the trouble with lies. Just tell one and then you have to tell a whole string of the beastly things, and before you know where you are, you've backed yourself into a corner with no way out. Perhaps this is why mothers always get quite beside themselves about lies. You can sulk, have tantrums, lose things, break things, even swear, but a lie is guaranteed to light the fuse of any mother however tolerant she may be under normal circumstances.

Chapter Four

 lmost as soon as Geoffrey had fallen asleep, old Mother Redpath's cockerel blasted the village awake with his self-important crowing. In fact, it sounded more like someone being strangled than the tidy "Cock-a-doodle-do" of a story-book fowl.

"Uk-a-aaaaargh!" it shrieked unpleasantly from the garden next door. "Uk-a-aaaaargh!"

"Oh, shut up," muttered Geoffrey crossly, as he dragged his aching limbs out of bed and groped around for his clothes, which were in a pathway of heaps from the side of his bed to the door. He followed the trail out of the room, pausing to put on the garments as he went.

His mother was already up and bustling about in the kitchen. It was amazing, the tasks she could accomplish with her arms and fingers held completely rigid in their splints. When Geoffrey entered the room he found her putting the kettle on the hob, holding it deftly between her stiff arms, rather as a Dutch doll might if it could. The fire was already blazing merrily. Goodness knows how she had managed that.

"Here's a nice egg on toast for you, my love," she cooed. "And a nice cup of tea to follow. I saved a bit of bread from Sir Walter's bag of food. It seemed wasteful just to eat it all at once. Anyway, you'll need a good breakfast to keep your strength up, walking all that way and doing a day's work. I can't tell you how proud I am, son. I shall be off round the village telling *everyone* the minute I've got my housework done."

"I wouldn't tell *everyone*," mumbled Geoffrey, feeling rather red in the face.

"Modest too!" smiled his mother.

The situation was growing worse every minute. Geoffrey munched miserably through his breakfast, as his joyful mother wrapped up the remaining morsels of Sir Walter's supper for her son's first working lunch.

If only she knew, thought Geoffrey, who was feeling more appalled every moment, like a person blundering on and on into a swamp.

Geoffrey left the house immediately after he had eaten, with the excuse that he had to be there by eight-thirty. He set off briskly down the lane, trying to convince himself that there was some way out of this ghastly mess without his mother finding out. He had actually walked a good eight miles of the journey when he realized that he had convinced himself that he was expected at the agency by eight-thirty. For a few moments, he felt a wave of relief that he was not expected anywhere, with the whole blue-skied day waiting unexplored in front of him. Then he remembered all the lies he had told and they settled like a lead weight over his heart. "One mile to Axington", read the next milestone which he passed.

Perhaps, thought Geoffrey in desperation, as the tower of Axington church appeared in the distance, perhaps if I just believe with all my heart that there will be a job at the agency, then perhaps there really will be! What was that saying about faith moving mountains or something? Anyway, I'll concentrate on it all the way there and perhaps they'll say "Come in, lad, you're just the person we're looking for. How would five shillings a week, plus luncheon vouchers and a company horse suit you?"

Forcing himself to feel confident, Geoffrey marched the last mile having wonderful fantasies about either becoming the managing director with a big leather chair, or being knighted the moment he walked into the office and rescuing a fair damsel on his first day. Actually, at eleven years old he was still a bit on the young side for damsel-rescuing. To tell the truth, he could see much more point in rescuing a kitten stuck up a tree than a silly old damsel in a tower, weeping into her embroidery. Still, if his friend Sir Walter was into damsel-rescuing, then that would certainly be the first item on Geoffrey's agenda.

A big wooden sign by the roadside read:

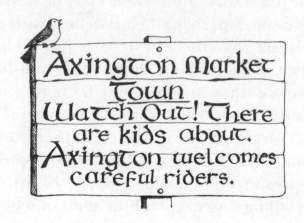

Axington Market Town
Watch Out! There are kids about.
Axington welcomes careful riders.

Axington was quite a small town, though it looked enormous to Geoffrey, who had lived all his life in Under-Withy-on-the-Marsh. Under-Withy was little more than a hamlet with only seven houses and not so much as a village store. You had to walk five miles to Under-Wallop-on-the-Hill if you wanted an evening news-sheet or a bag of groceries.

Geoffrey guessed that it must be market day by the unusual crowds thronging the streets. There were people everywhere, nearly all of them pushing trolleys, wheelbarrows and even baskets on wheels overflowing with garden produce – lettuces, onions and so on. Herds of cattle, flocks of geese and sheep, and grunting litters of pigs were being prodded noisily along by boys with sticks, and every now and then an ox-cart lumbered by, groaning beneath sacks of vegetables, bales of hay and naughty children hanging off the back for fun.

Geoffrey threaded his way through the busy crowds to Old Barrow Street. This was a narrow side-street crammed with houses of many different shapes and sizes, all listing drunkenly to one side like a shelf of books leaning up against a book-end. He knew where the agency was, for he had often passed by when visiting the town in the hope of glimpsing one of the knights riding out of the yard.

Geoffrey stopped outside one of the houses, which was painted a delicate shade of pink with an overhanging upper storey. Next to the front door was a neat brass plaque upon which was engraved:

FREELANCE RESCUE SERVICES LTD
OFFICES FIRST FLOOR
STABLEYARD THROUGH ARCHWAY
ON RIGHT

Geoffrey decided to try his luck in the stableyard first, and see if, by some extraordinary coincidence, a stable-lad had just been given the sack, died, or stormed off in a huff. He walked through the chilly passageway and out into the large square yard which had loose-boxes all the way round with their upper doors clipped back. An elderly man in worn leather clothes was coming out of one of the stables with an armful of bridles.

"Clear off, you!" he snarled at Geoffrey with unnecessary venom. "Be off now or I'll set Mauler on you."

A blood-curdling volley of barks and growls burst forth from one of the loose-boxes, which obviously imprisoned the ferocious Mauler. Geoffrey backed hastily out of the yard.

"I was just wondering," he called out as he went, "if you needed a stable-hand."

"If I need any stable-hands, it won't be you I'll be asking," growled the man. "Anyway, we've got enough stable-hands here to last the next twenty years. Now clear off. Go on, hop it! Stupid kids hanging round here all day, getting in the way, pinching things..." He trailed off, still muttering, through a door in the corner.

Geoffrey felt dreadfully embarrassed and rather hurt at the man's rudeness. It seemed as if he had taken a violent dislike to Geoffrey in person. (In fact, he was like it to everyone, even the knights, but Geoffrey wasn't to know that.) Also, if that had been the reaction of the stableman, then the office people would probably be even worse. The church clock chimed nine, and Geoffrey decided to wander about in the market for a while before he braved the office staff.

Chapter Five

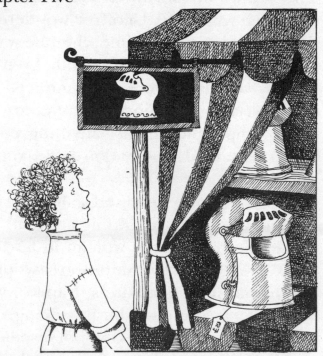

n hour dragged by as Geoffrey sauntered aimlessly through the bustling throng, wishing that he had some money in his pocket, for the stalls were all laden with the most interesting goods. There were clothing-stalls, hat-stalls, armour-stalls full of breast-plates and helmets glinting in the morning sunshine, vegetable-stalls, huge dusty pens of lowing cattle, and, every now

and then, a food-stall which was the medieval equivalent of a café. Geoffrey wondered if there would ever be a time when he wasn't constantly thinking about food. Even his dreams at night were of banquets and breakfast tables groaning with buttered toast, bacon, apple pie, in fact anything edible which his starved imagination could conjure up.

He stopped outside a food-stall with a jolly red and white striped awning above it. The stall-holder was a large woman in a scarlet dress covered by a voluminous, greasy apron. She had a white head-dress draped round her scarlet face and was busily stoking a fire which had a gigantic cooking-pot suspended over it. On the table beneath the awning was a mouth-watering array of cooked chicken pieces, buttered rolls, cakes of every description, a huge basket of apples and pears, and several pewter jugs filled with a fruit drink which had large chunks of fruit floating about in it.

"Can I help for a while?" asked Geoffrey hopefully. "I wondered if I might help for a bit, in exchange for a roll and a piece of chicken?"

The red-faced lady looked as if she was going to snap at him, but she changed her mind. "You can peel this lot for a roll, and *one* bit of chicken, mind," she said, pointing to a vast stack of potatoes underneath the table.

"What, *all* of them?" exclaimed Geoffrey, sounding horrified.

"Take it or leave it. They'll get done anyway," said the woman, flinging a bowlful of chopped onions into the cooking pot and stirring vigorously.

"I'll do them," said Geoffrey, wondering if it might not have been better to go hungry rather than hack his way through forty pounds of potatoes.

The stall-holder handed him a knife and two of the largest saucepans he had ever seen, and he sat on the floor and commenced peeling. At first he was very careful, taking several minutes per potato. After twenty minutes the pile still looked exactly the same, so he speeded up, cutting off such large chunks that the stallholder noticed and shouted down at him.

"Oy!" she bellowed as she wrapped a chicken-leg for a customer. "Watch what you're doing down there. You're taking off half the potato with the skin. Come on, I'd best be doing them myself."

"No, no!" said Geoffrey, visions of the promised food dancing before his eyes. "I'll be more careful, honestly I will. Look!" And he began peeling again with exaggerated care.

After another twenty minutes he almost began to enjoy it. There was a certain grim satisfaction in watching the earthy brown pile reducing, while both the massive saucepans began to fill up. In the end it took him exactly two and a half hours to the last potato.

"I've done them!" he shrieked, jumping to his feet and flexing his hand at the wrists where they felt as if they might drop off altogether.

The stall-holder peered at the saucepans. "Well," she said, smiling broadly, much to Geoffrey's relief. "I must admit, that *has* been a help. Here you are then, a leg of chicken, a roll and butter *and* a rock-cake for good measure."

It was now lunch-time. The town clock was striking twelve, and there was quite a queue of people at the stall. As Geoffrey stood eating his hard-earned food, the man from the stall next door (which sold leather bags, belts and boots) called across to him in a friendly way.

"I was watching you, sitting down there," he said to Geoffrey. "Great pile of 'em, wasn't there? Bet you're glad that's over."

"Mmmm," agreed Geoffrey, gnawing at the last remnants of the chicken-bone.

"Looking for a job then?" asked the man.

"Yes, I am, as a matter of fact," replied

Geoffrey. "I'm just off to the Freelance Rescue agency to see about a job there."

"Well, fancy that!" exclaimed the man. "What a coincidence. The secretary there just happens to be my fiancée. Are you going there this minute?"

"When I've finished this cake," said Geoffrey, cramming the whole thing into his mouth and nearly choking on the crumbs.

"Take it easy, lad," said the man, as Geoffrey coughed and spluttered. "Goodness, I've never seen anyone eat so fast. Now then. Will you take a note to the agency for me? My fiancée's name is Matilda. She's the only secretary there, so you can't miss her. And

she's wearing a big ruby engagement ring –
well actually, it's only glass, but it *looks* like a
ruby. Anyway, she'll be wearing it. Would
you do that for me?"

Geoffrey nodded, his eyes still watering
from the coughing fit. The man wrote a
hasty note, which he rolled into a scroll and
tied with a leather bootlace. He also pulled
an apple from his pocket and tossed both
the note and the apple across the counter.

"Here, catch!" he said. Geoffrey missed
and had to crawl about on his hands and
knees to retrieve them from beneath the
food-stall.

"Thank you, sir," he said, tucking the
scroll into his shirt and the apple into his
pocket. "I'll be off this minute."

When he reached the agency at Old
Barrow Street, Geoffrey boldly marched up
the front steps and pushed open the heavy
front door, before he had time to get
nervous. Inside there was a table with a vase
of wilting flowers on it, and a wooden notice
on the wall, with an arrow pointing up the
winding staircase. The notice read:
FREELANCE RESCUE SERVICES LTD.
ENQUIRIES – FIRST FLOOR.

Opposite the notice was a door upon which was stencilled COPY ROOM. The door was slightly ajar, and Geoffrey could see two young women bent over an enormous table, writing busily with quill pens. The table was piled high with bundles of paper all clipped neatly together, bunches of quill pens stuffed into jars and dozens of pots of different coloured inks.

Geoffrey climbed the staircase to the next floor. Here he was confronted by a small landing and a door with FREELANCE RESCUE SERVICES LTD printed on it in gold letters. ENQUIRIES – PLEASE KNOCK, said a smaller notice fixed to the wall. Geoffrey knocked.

"Enter!" called a cheerful voice from inside.

Geoffrey's heart lifted at the sound of the welcoming voice, and he opened the door and went in.

Chapter Six

eoffrey found himself in an extremely cluttered office. Three of the walls were covered from floor to ceiling with shelves, all so heavily laden with books and files that it seemed a miracle they were still attached to the brackets. The fourth wall was completely covered by a cage, divided into literally hundreds of pigeon-holes. Some of the holes were empty and others contained sulky looking pigeons, either asleep or preening their feathers. There were labels on each pigeon-hole displaying the name of a town, such as "Bristol (western area)" or "London (eastern end)". There was a small hole in

each cage which led to the outside world. Geoffrey imagined how draughty the office must be in the winter, though on such a sweltering day it provided a pleasant cooling breeze. In the centre of the room was an enormous desk almost hidden under an untidy mass of filing trays, envelopes, papers, an abacus, quill pens in holders, ink-pots, a three-branched candlestick, and even a bag of sandwiches.

Geoffrey could only just see the top half of the lady who had told him to enter. She glanced up over gold half-spectacles, her face framed by a wimple (which is a sort of

scarf wrapped round the head that ladies often wore) and one of those tall pointed hats topped by a veil which were the height of fashion in those days.

As Geoffrey approached the desk a huge dog sprang out unexpectedly from the knee-hole, barking and jumping up playfully. It was attached to a piece of stout rope which was in turn tied to the desk leg, but as the rope was ridiculously long and could have walked the dog at least three times round the desk, it was no use at all for keeping the creature under control. Closer inspection by Geoffrey revealed that it was an over-sized puppy, with shaggy dark fur, a long wolfy nose, small circular golden eyes rather like a teddy bear's, and a tail of inordinate length and furriness which created such a draught with its wagging that papers and envelopes fluttered to the floor in the breeze.

"Lancelot!" called the lady. "Stop it at *once*! Get down!"

Lancelot took no notice at all and proceeded to prance and twirl round the visitor, until the lady emerged from behind the desk and whacked the leaping puppy smartly with a rolled-up scroll of papers.

This brought Lancelot to his senses and he slunk back under the desk in a tangle of rope, paws and tail.

"Sorry about that," said the lady, settling back into her seat behind the desk. "Now then, may I help you?"

"Um – well, yes, actually," said Geoffrey vaguely. "I just thought, well, I was wondering if you might possibly have any jobs going, perhaps?"

The secretary laughed. "*Oh* dear," she said. "I'm afraid there are no jobs available at the moment. I'm the permanent secretary. We have two copy-scribes *and* all the stable-hands we can manage – added to which there's a waiting-list as long as your arm for everything, so there really *isn't* any chance at all, I'm afraid."

"Don't you need a messenger-boy?" asked Geoffrey.

"We've already got two," said the secretary. "*And* a good service of carrier-pigeons to every part of the country."

Geoffrey looked miserably at his feet. "Tea-boy?" he asked brightly.

The secretary smiled sympathetically. "*I'm* usually the tea-boy," she said, getting up. "Now off you go. As far as I can see, there won't be any jobs here before the next century."

She pushed back her chair and Geoffrey caught sight of a brilliant red ring flashing on her finger.

"Oh, I've just remembered!" he exclaimed, fishing about inside his shirt and drawing out the scroll, which was somewhat flattened from being squashed against his chest. "I've brought a message for you."

"For *me*?" asked the secretary, looking baffled.

"You *are* Matilda, aren't you?" asked

Geoffrey, handing her the scroll. "I met your fiancé in the market, and he told me that you were the secretary here and asked if I would deliver this."

"Well, thank you very much, lad," said Matilda, untying the bootlace and beginning to read.

At this point, there did not seem to be any reason for Geoffrey to remain hanging about. "Goodbye, then," he said politely, opening the door.

Matilda held up her hand. "Wait a moment, would you?" she said. "I *might* have a little job for you after all. How would you like to mind the office while everyone's at lunch? Simon – that's my fiancé – says he'll treat me to lunch if I can get away for an hour. One of us always stays in the office in case of an emergency, and it's my turn today. What do you think?"

"I think it's a great idea!" said Geoffrey. "Just tell me what I have to do."

"Well," said Matilda, "first of all, you'd better nip out and wait in the doorway opposite. Sir Cedric – he's the boss – I think he'd be a bit annoyed at me leaving a stranger in charge. Not that anything ever happens at lunch-time; in fact I don't know why they insist on it, really. I've been here for five years now and nothing's ever happened, not once. Anyway, you just wait out of sight till you see the two copy-scribes leave, and Sir Cedric. He'll be off to his club.

"When it's all clear, come back up and I'll tell you what to do. Sir Cedric never gets back till three and he's always tiddly. Anyway, I'll be back within the hour, so you'll have nothing to worry about. Off you go now, quickly! I can hear Sir Cedric moving about in his office!"

Geoffrey clattered excitedly down the stairs

and found a conveniently shaded doorway across the road in which to lurk. Within five minutes Sir Cedric came out.

He was very old, with a white moustache so long that it wafted in the breeze on either side of him like a scarf.

He had a pronounced limp and leaned heavily on a stick as he stumped off up the road. Next came the two copy-scribes, laughing and chattering.

Geoffrey raced back up the stairs to find Matilda applying rouge to her cheeks with the aid of a tiny mirror balanced on top of a filing-cabinet.

"I'll be off then," she said. "You can have the sandwiches I brought, if you like. Oh, and I'll give you a penny when I get back."

"Gosh, thanks!" gasped Geoffrey, wondering what fillings were in the sandwiches. He was also thrilled about the penny, which was a lot of money in those days.

"Now, all you have to do is keep an eye on the pigeons' cages in case of any messages," said Matilda, whose cheeks glowed so rosily that she looked as if she had scarlet fever. "I won't be long."

As she opened the door, Lancelot launched himself from beneath the desk.

"Oh, dear," said Matilda, pushing him down. "I'd forgotten about you." She turned to Geoffrey. "He really is a nuisance, this dog. I'm looking after him for my mother and it's a real bind bringing him to the office every day. Do you think you could keep him here while I'm out? He'll settle down and sleep once I've gone and he'd be such a pain in the market."

"Of course," said Geoffrey.

Chapter Seven

hen she had gone, and after he had bundled the exuberant Lancelot back under the desk with stern warnings to stay put, Geoffrey could not resist sneaking next door to have a look at Sir Cedric's office.

It was much tidier than Matilda's room, more like a study. There was a huge, dark green studded-leather armchair, and a leather swivel-chair behind a beautifully polished leather-topped desk. The desk was so brand-new and tidy that it did not look as if any work had ever been carried out on it at all. (In fact, very little work *was* carried out on it. Sir Cedric spent most of his time snoozing, reading the racing news-sheet or knocking back whisky at his club.) A brass ear-trumpet was laid out neatly next to a quill pen, a crystal ink-bottle (with no ink in it), a large leather-bound appointments diary and a framed portrait of a rotund and rather grim-faced lady, who was in fact Sir Cedric's wife.

All round the walls were paintings of knights. There were portraits of knights, knights *on* horseback, knights *off* horseback, knights slaying dragons and shinning up towers with damsels waving at the top, and there was even a group portrait of all the Freelance knights sitting together in a row (rather like a school photograph) with Sir Cedric in the centre, looking very ancient and venerable.

One wall was entirely given over to certificates of merit, with coloured rosettes and seals dangling from them. The room gave the impression of a cross between a successful riding establishment and an art-gallery.

Geoffrey backed out and sat down at Matilda's desk. To his absolute joy, he suddenly realized that he was still clutching the bag of sandwiches. Even better, he remembered the apple given to him by Matilda's fiancé which was still in his pocket. The sandwiches were cheese and pickle – big doorsteppy ones with slabs of cheese and chunks of pickle. He demolished them at once, followed by the apple, and sat back with his feet up on the desk.

This is the life, he thought happily, marvelling at the astonishing amount of food which had come his way in the last few hours. Why, he even had a penny wages to come later, enough to buy a decent supper for himself and his mother. Perhaps he could tell her how he'd made up the whole story about getting a job at the agency, and perhaps she wouldn't be so cross if she happened to be in the middle of a nice steak-and-kidney pie.

As he sat there day-dreaming, a sudden flurry in the pigeon-cage brought him back to reality. A rather wind-ruffled pigeon had bustled through one of the holes in the wall into its cage and was busily cooing and stretching its wings, while the other pigeons all cooed and clucked and bustled about on their perches.

Geoffrey was a bit nervous of birds. His mother had once kept some ferocious hens which used to pursue him round the garden every time he ventured out.

He cautiously opened the cage door and

the pigeon sprang at the opening in a great flurry of beating wings, scratching claws and pecking beak. Geoffrey jumped backwards and the bird launched itself through the opening and proceeded to fly madly round the room, bashing into shelves and piles of papers while the other birds squawked and fluttered in their cages, like prisoners encouraging an inmate who has escaped. The dreadful puppy joined in gleefully, leaping up to try to catch the bird, and knocking over a large potted plant and a bottle of black ink as it did so.

After several futile minutes of careering round the room grabbing nervously at the fugitive pigeon, Geoffrey realized that it would be best to keep still and let it settle.

"Get *down*, Lancelot!" he bellowed, swatting the delinquent dog with a copy of *The Carrier Pigeon Directory for Eastern England*.

Lancelot was in such a state of hysteria that Geoffrey had to sit on him to calm him down. Terrified that someone might hear and come to investigate the barking, he seized the puppy's long snout and held his jaws firmly together. Lancelot stopped struggling and gazed up indignantly at Geoffrey with bright amber-coloured eyes.

"Sorry, Lance," whispered Geoffrey. "But you *must* be quiet."

After what seemed like five hours, but was in fact ten minutes, the pigeon calmed down and roosted on the candelabra, which was suspended from the ceiling.

The room looked as if a bomb had hit it. The floor was littered with papers, the broken plant all jumbled up with the earth from the plant-pot, a knocked-over chair and, worst of all, an appalling black ink-stain caused by the overturned ink-bottle, which was still dripping steadily down the side of the desk on to the carpet. A few feathers drifted gently through the air like the beginning of a snow shower.

Geoffrey felt a lurch of horror as he surveyed the scene. He righted the ink-bottle and picked up the chair, but the whole office appeared to be wrecked. Even the calendar on the wall had fallen off its hook. Indeed, it was hard to imagine that one measly pigeon had been the cause of such a riot.

The measly pigeon was now happily settled on the candelabra, preening its tail feathers. Geoffrey could see the wooden carrier attached to its leg like a tiny splint. Moving very slowly, he climbed on to the chair and lunged at the unsuspecting pigeon, just catching it as it took off.

"Got you!" he yelled in triumph, not even caring that it was pecking and scratching him. Lancelot leapt up, barking and jumping again, so that all the pigeons in the cages commenced squawking and leaping about on their perches. The noise was awful, but Geoffrey did not notice for the moment as he was busily removing the piece of paper from the message-holder. Once he had done this, he suddenly noticed that the pigeon was pecking away at his hands, and hastily let it go. It flew back to the candelabra, where it sat in a hunched and sulky huddle.

Geoffrey was not too brilliant at reading and he had great difficulty in making out what the message said. He was not helped by the fact that the writer was not too brilliant at spelling either. The message said:

SEND REEENFORSMENTS
SIR WOLTER HAS ~~BIN~~
BEEN ~~BOPPED~~ ~~BORED~~
~~BOPPT~~ NOKKT ON
THE HED BY THE
EEVIL OGER GROBB
HOO WILL EET HIM
IF WE ARE NOT KWIK
PLEES SEND MOR
~~NITES~~ ~~KNITS~~ NIGHTS
TO SAVE HIS LORDSHIP
HE IS IN THE OGERS
KAVE SEND HELP AT WUNS

All Geoffrey's brainpower was needed to decipher this message. He sat down on the chair, frowning with concentration and tried desperately to work it out. At first he thought "REEENFORSMENTS" was refreshments. Then he saw "SIR WOLTER" on the next line and realized that it was his Sir Walter. "NOKKT ON THE HED" was not too difficult as this was how Geoffrey would have spelt it himself. The next part about the "EEVIL OGER GROBB" was fairly simple, but he got a bit stuck on the crossed-out "NITES" and "KNITS", mistaking "NITES" for nighties, knits for some sort of knitting and nights as something to do with night-time.

"This is very odd, Lancelot," he said to the puppy, who was lying on Geoffrey's feet, his tail draped in the inky patch on the carpet. "It says something about an ogre eating Sir Walter and we have to send nighties or knitting and refreshments at night. That can't be right can it?"

Rereading the note, letter by letter, it gradually dawned on Geoffrey that refreshments was in fact reinforcements and "NIGHTS" referred to knights of the armoured variety.

"Good heavens, Lancelot!" he gasped. "Sir Walter is about to be eaten by the evil Grobb that he told me about. How dreadful! I must go and get Matilda at once."

He leapt to his feet and rushed to the door. Lancelot sprang after him, nearly strangling himself on the rope and spraying ink from his tail all over the place.

"Oh, come on, then," said Geoffrey. "I s'pose I'll have to take you with me." He untied the rope from the desk leg and, with the other end wound several times round his hand and arm, they set off down the steep staircase. That is to say Lancelot set off down the staircase, dragging Geoffrey behind him like a waterskier.

eoffrey had hoped that Matilda and her fiancé would be at the food-stall next to her fiancé's leather shop, but they were not. Padlocked wooden shutters were drawn across the stall with a notice saying "Gone to lunch".

"Excuse me," said Geoffrey, tugging nervously at the food-stall owner's sleeve.

"Oh it's you, is it?" said the woman, who looked hot and flustered, and was still serving a queue of people.

"Have you seen the man from the leather-stall?" asked Geoffrey.

"He's gone to lunch," snapped the woman, ladling out a plateful of stew for a customer.

"Can't you read? There's a notice up. 'Gone to lunch', it says."

"I just wondered if you knew *where* he'd gone to lunch," persisted Geoffrey. "He had a lady with him."

"Look, sonny," said the woman, who was obviously having a hot, busy, unpleasant day, and did not feel in the least bit grateful about the potatoes. "I don't care if he had the *Queen* with him. He could be in Outer *Siberia* for all I know. OK?"

Embarrassed, Geoffrey slunk away into the crowd, dragging Lancelot with him. Lancelot was no help at all. The only thing that interested him was investigating all the rubbish in the gutters.

Geoffrey looked in half-heartedly at another food-stall several streets away, then decided that there was no alternative but to go and help Sir Walter himself. "SEND HELP AT WUNS!" the message had said. Why, Sir Walter might even now be part of Grobb's lunch.

He looked about him and saw an ancient donkey and cart tethered to a vegetable-stall. The owner had just removed a large sack of carrots and was heaving it inside.

Geoffrey hastily untied the donkey's reins and jumped on to the seat, hauling Lancelot up beside him. "Gee up!" he bawled.

The donkey appeared to be stone deaf and did not even twitch an ear, let alone begin to move, but the owner heard and bellowed at Geoffrey.

"Oy! You young oik! Get down off there this minute or you'll be sorry!"

"*Please* gee up!" pleaded Geoffrey, flapping the reins feebly across the donkey's back.

Still the donkey did not move and it was Lancelot who came to the rescue with a volley of high-pitched barking. This startled the ancient creature, and set it off through

the streets with such a jerk that Geoffrey and Lancelot fell backwards off the seat into the body of the cart. The last thing Geoffrey heard above the clattering of hoofs and cartwheels was the angry yelling of the donkey's rightful owner, who pursued them until he was too out of breath to run any more.

The donkey took the road towards Rowanbank as it sped out of Axington. By an incredibly convenient twist of fate, it happened to live in the village just beyond Rowanbank (a small village named St Nonny) and was extremely keen to get home and have its bucket of oats. Geoffrey did not

know this, of course, and, once he had regained his position on the driver's seat, he felt rather proud of his driving skills; the donkey trotted briskly along the road, needing no encouragement. Lancelot sat happily in the back and barked at everything in sight including the butterflies.

"Oh, *do* stop it, Lance," said Geoffrey crossly. "You're giving me a headache. Anyway, I've got some serious thinking to do."

The first thing, he decided, was to call in at his mother's house to see if he could find a suitable weapon. He also intended to ask his mother to "babysit" for Lancelot, who would obviously be a fat lot of use in the task ahead.

It was early evening as the little cart creaked into Under-Withy-on-the-Marsh. The donkey was now grimly determined to get back to his home village, and Geoffrey had quite a struggle to rein him to a halt and tie him to the gatepost. Having done this he raced up the path with Lancelot flat out in front of him.

Geoffrey's mother was sitting in the rocking-chair with a cup of tea on the table in front of her.

"Good gracious, Geoffrey!" she exclaimed, as Lancelot sprang joyously into her lap and began slurping the tea. "Get down, you brute!" She pushed him off. "What on earth is all this, Geoffrey? How could you bring a dog home at a time like this when we haven't a penny in the house? And a great bouncing useless brute at that."

"I'm on an assignment, Mother," explained Geoffrey. "I have to rush over to Rowanbank to rescue Sir Walter – you know, the one who shared his supper with me.

He's got captured by this ogre, only I forgot to bring any weapons with me. *Have* we got anything?"

"An assignment?" echoed his mother, looking alarmed. "All by yourself? Is it *usual* to be sent on an assignment on your first day – without any training? And an ogre! Isn't there someone with you – a bit bigger, perhaps?"

"Oh, don't fuss, Mother. They said I was a natural," boasted Geoffrey, almost believing it to be true. "The managing director *himself* sent me. 'See to it lad,' he said to me. 'Just do whatever's necessary to get our Walter back!'"

"Well I never!" said Geoffrey's mother, trying to see her son in a new light, though he still looked very small and youthful to her. "Well then, I suppose we'd better find you some weapons, though I must say I can't think of anything that will be much use."

They searched through the house and came up with a very odd assortment of household equipment which looked as if it might be useful as weaponry. There was a toasting-fork, a warming-pan, the poker, a pair of fire-tongs, a small kitchen-knife, the bread-knife and several pairs of quite deadly-looking wooden knitting needles.

They also found a small weeding-fork in the front garden. Lancelot sneaked off behind a chair with one of the knitting-needles and proceeded to chew it to pieces while no one was looking.

"It's not much, is it?" said Geoffrey's mum, surveying the heap of weapons on the carpet.

"I suppose you could fill the warming-pan with hot coals and swing it at your foe. Or you could grab them by the throat with the tongs – though if it's an ogre, you'd need a step-ladder to get up to his throat in the first place. We've *got* an old step-ladder in the shed. Would you like to take it?"

"Don't be daft, Mum," said Geoffrey. "An ogre would have to be pretty stupid not to notice me propping up a step-ladder against him. I can hardly say, 'Excuse me, old chap, do you mind if I just shin up this ladder and grab you with my tongs?' now can I?"

"No, I suppose you can't," mused his mother.

"I'll take the poker and one of these fat knitting-needles," said Geoffrey. "The kitchen-knife looks a bit – well, horrid really, doesn't it?"

"Isn't it *supposed* to look horrid?" asked Geoffrey's mum.

"The poker looks quite horrid enough to me," said Geoffrey, turning pale at the thought of even squashing an ant, let alone assaulting anyone with the kitchen-knife. "By the way, I must take some water out to my transport."

His mother was somewhat alarmed when she saw the rickety donkey-cart tied to the gatepost. "Good heavens, boy, is *that* your transport?" she exclaimed. "An old cart with a bag of bones to pull it?"

"There's nothing wrong with this fellow," said Geoffrey, setting down a bucket of water for the animal. "He can't wait to be off again. Now, Mum, could you be a saint and look after Lancelot for me till I get back? Where is he by the way?"

They hurried back inside and discovered Lancelot standing on the kitchen table where he had knocked over a jug of milk and was wading about in it, trying to lick it up before it all cascaded on to the floor. He wagged his tail happily at them as they came in, but did not bother to look up until Geoffrey's mother let out a murderous shriek.

"On second thoughts," said Geoffrey, noting the expression on her face, "I'll take him with me." He grabbed the rope, which was trailing in the milk, and pulled Lancelot off the table.

"You really are a hopeless case, dog, d'you know that?" he said crossly, yanking him out of the house and down the path.

"Goodbye then, son," said his mother, as she watched him climb into the cart with the poker and knitting-needle stuck bravely in his belt. "I'm sure you'll be all right. Come by on your way back and tell me what happened won't you? Don't forget now."

"I'll bring Sir Walter himself to tell you," promised Geoffrey, as Lancelot jumped up beside him. "Would you untie the reins for me?"

His mother untied the reins and tossed them up to him, but before they reached his hands, the donkey had set off at a cracking pace, homeward bound for St Nonny and his bucket of oats. Geoffrey waved until his mother was out of sight.

Chapter Nine

 olting and rattling his way along the dirt road, Geoffrey grew steadily more anxious as he contemplated the awful task ahead of him. He also felt decidedly uncomfortable when he remembered the appalling state in which he had left the office. He imagined Matilda returning from lunch, to be confronted by the vandalized room, and with a sinking heart he realized that it would look as if he was an irresponsible hooligan who had ransacked the room, let the pigeon out and stolen the dog just for fun. Worse still, he imagined Matilda being hauled into Sir Cedric's office and being sacked for leaving the place in charge of a total stranger.

Sifting through these dismal thoughts, Geoffrey's shoulders hunched up round his ears and he looked the picture of misery. Even Lancelot seemed a bit glum, resting his furry nose on Geoffrey's knee, and for the first time Geoffrey felt glad that the puppy was with him.

"You're not *so* bad, Lance old boy," he said kindly. "It won't take us five minutes to get Sir Walter back, will it?"

He prattled on in this way to the puppy, who gave every appearance of listening intently, and by the time the little party creaked into Rowanbank, Geoffrey felt quite confident that he would know *exactly* what to do when the time came. Just *what* he would do was another question, but he felt sure he would think of something later.

Behind the wonky village roof-tops, the sun was setting in a spectacular blaze of pinks and reds. Geoffrey had expected the village to be crowded with anxious people milling about awaiting reinforcements, but the place seemed to be completely deserted. Halfway down the main street a door slowly opened about two inches, and Geoffrey could see half a suspicious-looking bearded face and a hand round the edge of the door.

"Pssst!" hissed the man. "You there! What d'you think you're doing? There's an ogre on the prowl!"

A hot blast of fear shot through Geoffrey's chest, as he came out of his day-dreams and realized that the evil Grobb might actually be lurking round the next corner. He reined in the donkey with great difficulty, for the poor creature knew that its home village was only half a mile away and was more determined than ever to get back. The only

way to stop was for Geoffrey to jump into the road and lean back against him while hanging on to the reins as tightly as he could. To make matters even worse, Lancelot had taken great exception to the man's furtive behaviour and had begun to bark frantically from his perch on the driver's seat. Being rather a nice dog at heart, he had grown very fond of Geoffrey in their short time together and decided that his new master needed defending from this gruff stranger.

"Lancelot, for heaven's *sake!*" exclaimed Geoffrey in exasperation, realizing what an incompetent picture he was presenting to the man behind the door: a small dishevelled boy, struggling to calm a difficult donkey and an unruly puppy. He tried to put on a serious, intelligent expression.

"We got your message about Sir Walter," he announced, trying to keep the nervous quaver out of his voice.

"Message?" queried the man, looking blank.

"The carrier-pigeon message," said Geoffrey. "I'm the reinforcements. Now then, my good man. Can you direct me to the ogre's lair?"

"Well, bless my soul!" exclaimed the man, opening the door another inch to get a better look. "Reinforcements, eh? Bit young, aren't you, son?"

"I just *look* young," said Geoffrey, feeling peeved at the man's lack of confidence in him. He had imagined the entire village turning out to cheer his arrival.

"How old *are* you?" asked the man suspiciously.

"I'm seventeen, as a matter of fact," said Geoffrey, embarrassed. "I qualified early at knight-school. Just because I'm small doesn't mean I'm not capable. Now, you'd better tell me where I can find this ogre's lair. Sir

Walter may be being eaten at this very moment."

"Where's your armour then?" asked the man, beginning to sound nasty.

"Look, this is ridiculous!" exclaimed Geoffrey. "Will you please just tell me where the ogre's lair is, or do I have to ask at another house? Lancelot, shut *up!*" He aimed a blow at Lancelot, who leapt into the back of the cart, looking deeply offended.

"Well, sonny," said the man, opening the door properly. "If you're *really* sure about this."

He stepped into the street and pointed to a hill rising steeply behind the village.

"See those wild-looking trees up there, lad?" he said, pointing to a clump of trees curved sideways by the wind, almost at the top of the hill. "Well, when you get up close, there's a cave just round to the right. That's the ogre's lair. He'll be lighting the fire for his dinner soon, so you should be able to spot it easily. He really is an *enormous* fellow, you know. At least twenty feet high and that dreadful eye rolling about. Gives me the shudders just thinking about it."

"Well, thanks for your help anyway," said

Geoffrey, trying to sound briskly confident. At the same moment, the struggling donkey gave an almighty lunge and bolted down the street. Geoffrey had to run flat out for several minutes before he caught up enough to jump aboard.

Lancelot was delighted to have his master back. He had barked encouragingly from the cart as Geoffrey had panted along behind, and now he pounced into his lap and began to wash him thoroughly.

"Get off!" ordered Geoffrey, shoving the whirling mass of ears, paws and pink tongue off the seat. "Just leave me alone for five minutes, can't you?"

Lancelot lay down flat like a sheep-dog, with his nose neatly between his paws, trying to look cute. Geoffrey didn't notice. He was too preoccupied with trying to get his breath back and wondering what on earth he was going to *do*.

The ogre's hill was closer to the village than it looked and they reached the foot of the hill within a quarter of an hour.

"This is *it*, Lance," said Geoffrey, feeling scared out of his wits. He dragged on the reins and managed to halt the determined donkey with much bucking and straining.

"Well then, boy," said Geoffrey, picking up Lancelot's rope and winding it round his hand. "Here we go."

Lancelot took this quite literally and leapt out at once, hauling Geoffrey several yards up the hillside behind him. The wily donkey swiftly took advantage of the situation and set off at a rate of knots. Geoffrey watched in horror as his getaway vehicle disappeared for ever in a cloud of dust.

"You *stupid* dog!" snapped Geoffrey, jerking the rope. "Sit *down*, you stupid, idiotic, mangy cur! You great lolloping *lump*! Look what you've done.

"Now we're *really* stuck, aren't we? Supposing we *do* manage to get Sir Walter free. How on earth do you think we're going to escape, with a twenty-foot ogre tearing down the hill after us, eh? Well?"

Lancelot, who was truly embarrassed as his master ranted and raved and waved a finger at him, tried all the puppy-tricks he knew to win Geoffrey round. First of all he sat down and hung his head as low as possible, turning up his golden eyes in a mournful way.

When this did not stem the flow of anger, he grovelled across the grass on his stomach and rested his head on Geoffrey's foot, with a tiny flicker of his tail.

This was not a proper wag, which would

have seemed disrespectful, but a fluttering of the tip of the tail, as if to say, "Please forgive me, so I can be happy again." He rounded it off by sitting bolt upright with his head held shamefacedly to one side, and waving a huge shaggy paw rather vaguely in Geoffrey's direction.

"*Sorry,* are you," said Geoffrey, feeling far less angry but not wanting to admit it. "I should think so too! Well, just you behave, d'you hear? No more barking or running off or we'll both find ourselves in a casserole. Do you understand me?"

Lancelot noted the softening of his master's voice and wagged his tail frantically with relief.

Still with no plan of action, Geoffrey began creeping up the hillside with Lancelot slinking along beside him like a model puppy, quite determined (for the moment, anyway) to be the best-behaved dog in the universe so that Geoffrey could feel proud of him.

Darkness had fallen and Geoffrey found it difficult to tell how far he had climbed. Stopping for a moment to peer upwards, his heart thumping so forcefully that he felt sure they could hear it back in the village, he saw a fire being lit only thirty yards away. It was so close, in fact, that Geoffrey could make out the shape of a monstrous figure casting awful flickering shadows as the flames leapt higher. Lancelot saw it too and opened his mouth to "see off" the enemy. Fortunately, Geoffrey heard the warning growl and seized him by the snout, clamping his jaws tightly shut.

"Ssssh, you idiot!" he whispered desperately into the puppy's ear. "You *must* listen to what I say! Please Lance, *don't* bark!"

Although Lancelot could not understand a word of all this, and every dog-instinct told him to rush menacingly towards the threatening shape while making as much noise as possible, there was a note of urgency in Geoffrey's voice which reduced him to silence. Geoffrey tentatively released the jaws and Lancelot drooped a contrite head on his master's knee.

"Good boy," whispered Geoffrey, at the same time suddenly feeling so frightened that his knees began to shake and he had to sit down on the ground. Lancelot sat down next to him and leaned his head tenderly across Geoffrey's pounding chest.

The ogre really *was* at least twenty feet tall.

It looked more like forty to the minuscule Geoffrey, but in fact was twenty-nine feet, seven and a quarter inches (which was quite tall enough). Geoffrey watched in fascinated horror as the fire blazed up, gradually giving more light until he could see only too clearly what he was up against.

He had never seen even a picture of an ogre before, so the sight of this ghastly creature was worse than he could possibly have imagined. For a start, the thing was scarcely human. It was more like a gigantic, stooping gorilla with a few human characteristics. In the centre of its wrinkled forehead was the one eye which everyone had told Geoffrey about. It was actually a human sort of eye with a bag underneath it and an eyebrow on top of it, but this only made matters worse, as the rest of the face was like a cross between an ape and an old potato. It had massive shoulders and long arms from which dangled huge claw-like hands, and it was covered from head to foot with rather moth-eaten-looking grey fur, except for its face. It was wearing no clothes at all. Somehow, Geoffrey had imagined that it would be exactly like a large man except for the one eye. He had even remembered Sir Walter's words about tact, and had envisaged persuading the ogre to sit down and have a reasonable discussion with him.

"Now look here, old bean," he would have said in a sincere voice. "This is all a bit silly really, isn't it? Why don't I just nip off and buy you a couple of oxen and a few sheep for your dinner in exchange for Sir Walter. How about that? Fair enough, eh?" But he could now see quite clearly that there would be no chance of any sort of discussion with this shambling monster.

The flames leapt higher and higher, lighting up the curved trees and the mouth of a cave in the rocks. The ogre hurled whole treetrunks on to the fire, its ghastly shadow stretching twice as large up the hillside behind it.

To Geoffrey, crouching in the darkness, it seemed as if he was watching a terrifying scene on a stage. The creature began to grunt and roar as it threw more fuel on to the blazing pyre.

Watching transfixed, Geoffrey had completely forgotten about Lancelot. The

roaring of the ogre proved too much for his dizzy puppy brain. Here was his new master beside him, and *there* was a decidedly threatening enemy making decidedly threatening noises. There was no doubt about it in Lancelot's mind: his master needed defending at once.

With a blood-curdling howl, he dashed forward, lips drawn back in as vicious-looking a snarl as he could manage. (Actually it wasn't vicious-looking at all. He was such a sweet-natured dog that it just made him look comical instead of nasty.)

Geoffrey watched in horror as the puppy rushed into the circle of light, barking frenziedly, fur standing on end like a wolf, and with the rope flying out behind him.

He looked so tiny darting around the

ogre's ankles, that Geoffrey closed his eyes and waited for the barking to be brought to an abrupt end by one of the hairy fists.

Then a wonderful thing happened.

Geoffrey cautiously opened one eye and

saw that the ogre had trodden on the end of the flailing rope. Lancelot had continued to twirl round the vast form until the rope tied its ankles together so suddenly that the huge monster toppled backwards. There was a terrible thud which shook the whole hillside as its head struck a rock at the entrance to the cave.

Geoffrey held his breath, but no sound came from the ogre, which lay where it had fallen with Lancelot attached to the side of its legs, yelping in that frantic way which puppies do whey they are frightened out of their wits. The high-pitched sound broke Geoffrey's trance and he jumped to his feet.

"It's all right, Lance, I'm coming!" he yelled, rushing towards
the firelight.
"Good boy!
Good dog!
It's all right!"

 uch to Geoffrey's relief, the ogre did not move at all as he worked to untie the rope from the collar round Lancelot's neck. Unfortunately, the knot was pulled very tight and there was only a short piece of rope free from the ogre's legs which meant that the poor dog's head was held flat against the ground. It did not help matters that Geoffrey's fingernails were bitten to the quick and Lancelot was so beside himself with fright that he kept trying to bite his rescuer.

"Stop it, Lance!" ordered Geoffrey, pulling his hands away to avoid the snapping white teeth. But poor Lancelot was in such a state that he was literally foaming at the mouth, and Geoffrey could see that it would be best to leave him for a few minutes to calm down rather than have all his fingers bitten off.

He wondered how much time he had before the ogre became conscious again, and crept cautiously along the side of the prostrate form until he was level with the repulsive head. The face was turned slightly away from him, with its one eye partially open. Geoffrey froze in his tracks when he noticed this, thinking that the ogre might be waking up, but there was not a flicker of movement from the eyelid. As Geoffrey peered at the thick neck, which was only lightly covered in fuzz, and the rope-like veins standing out on the taut surface, it occurred to him that they were not pulsing as veins usually did. The more he looked, the more he noticed that nothing was moving at all. The chest was not rising up and down, the eyelid was not fluttering, there was not a single twitch or sign of life anywhere. In fact the only thing moving was Lancelot, who continued to flap about next to the ogre's leg like an exhausted fish out of water.

Moving very slowly, Geoffrey nervously prodded the ogre's shoulder. There was no reaction, so he stood on tiptoe and felt around on the side of the head for an ear. There was a small crumpled ear lurking beneath the shaggy fur. Geoffrey pushed the fur aside, screamed into the ear as loudly as he could, and jumped back hastily in case the monster suddenly rose up roaring; but it didn't. Geoffrey edged his way forward again and gingerly placed his foot on the somewhat springy ear. Using it as a foothold, he hoisted himself on to the face, where he knelt down next to one of the cavernous nostrils.

This was extremely brave of him, considering the fact that the ogre might have been bluffing, and flipped him into its mouth with one swift movement. Using both hands, Geoffrey pushed the eyelid right back and saw that the eye had rolled up into the head. He turned to the nostrils and held his hands up to feel for the breath. Considering the size of the brute, its breath should have been like a hurricane. There was not even a breeze. There was no breath at all.

"Oh Lancelot!" gasped Geoffrey to the squealing puppy. "It's dead!" Then he burst into tears.

This took him completely by surprise, for it swept up inside him like a sudden storm, and he sat down on the ogre's cheek and cried like a small child, open-mouthed and knuckling away at his eyes to try to make himself stop.

But it didn't stop for quite a few minutes. The tears spurted from his eyes like a fountain, partly out of sheer relief that he was safe, and partly out of horror that anything at all (let alone anything quite so large) should have been killed.

Then he began to laugh when he thought about the worst trained dog in the universe killing the most feared ogre in the land. This odd mixture of laughter and tears is in fact the true meaning of hysterics, which is when you are so shocked or upset that your emotions get all jumbled up and you aren't quite sure whether whatever has happened is sad or funny.

Geoffrey finally pulled himself together and scrambled down to the ground, extremely glad that there was no one to see him. Lancelot was quieter. He was whining in a pitiful way, but the frenzy seemed to have passed, and he turned his eyes gratefully towards Geoffrey as he saw him coming.

"Easy, boy," said Geoffrey soothingly as he knelt down and struggled with the knot again. But it really was no use. His nails were non-existent and the knot would have to be cut. As he pulled and tugged, wishing he had a sword, he suddenly remembered Sir Walter.

Sir Walter! That's why he was there! To rescue Sir Walter. He had actually forgotten all about him during the excitement.

"It's all right, Lance," he said, his voice still trembling. "I'll be back in a minute. Don't worry now."

He ran to the mouth of the cave and peered in. It was pitch dark, so he went to the fire and pulled out a branch which had just caught alight, and took it with him as a torch.

The entrance led into a tunnel. It smelt dreadful, which was hardly surprising as the floor was littered with suspiciously human-looking bones and bits of indefinable carcasses. Geoffrey could hardly believe how brave he was being. He felt as if he were dreaming, holding his nose with one hand and the torch with the other.

"Sir Walter!" he called, his voice echoing

in a sinister way from the damp, rocky walls. "Sir Walter! Are you in here?"

The tunnel opened out into a chamber which was in an even worse state than the passage. It was literally knee-deep in evil-smelling bones, and in one corner was a pile of rotting vegetation which was obviously the ogre's bed.

"Sir Walter!" called Geoffrey, holding the flaming branch high above his head.

Beginning to lose heart, he was moving slowly round the grisly chamber examining every crevice and pile of bones, when he saw something move.

Whatever it was, it was completely hidden from view underneath a particularly nauseating pile of rotting matter. As he watched, the surface of the pile gave a slight swell, like a breathing chest. In fact it only moved once and so slightly that if Geoffrey had not been looking in that direction at the time he might never have seen it.

He hurried over and stuck the lighted branch into a rib-cage which was conveniently jammed between two boulders. He was so excited that he was not in the least bit unnerved by the awfulness of the bones as he scrabbled at the putrid-smelling mess. A few inches down, his hand struck something metallic. He scooped away several more handfuls and uncovered the breastplate of a suit of armour, tightly bound with creeper.

"*Please* let it be him," said Geoffrey under his breath. He scraped and pulled desperately at the leaves, grass and goodness knows what else until the whole head came into view. It was still wearing a helmet, with the visor closed. Hardly daring to breathe, Geoffrey pushed it back.

The face beneath was spattered with dirt which had fallen in through the breathing-slits, but there was no mistaking the laugh-lines round the eyes, the straight nose and the sky-blue eyes which opened blinking against the dirt and the torchlight.

"Oh, Sir Walter! Thank heavens you're all right," exclaimed Geoffrey, feeling, to his dismay, another tidal wave of tears sweep over him. But before he had time to start apologizing, Geoffrey was astonished to see tears begin streaming from Sir Walter's eyes, making long streaks down his dirty cheeks and dripping into the back of his helmet. This was the last straw for Geoffrey, who gave up all attempts to be brave and manly, and the two of them grizzled away unashamedly for several moments.

After a while they both stopped. "I'll have you out in a jiff, sir," sniffed Geoffrey, wiping his nose on his sleeve, which was the only thing available.

"Bless you," croaked Sir Walter weakly. "God bless you."

"I'm sorry to cry, sir," said Geoffrey, examining the creeper, which was tied in the most complicated way. "It's just – well, I thought you might be dead."

Sir Walter smiled. "So did I," he said good-humouredly. "It's a mercy this visor was down. It held the worst of all this muck off my face, so I could breathe. Can you get me out of here? Am I tied up? Is that why I can't move?"

"I'm afraid you are, sir," said Geoffrey. "You're tied up with creeper and the knots are very tight. I haven't got a knife, sir, and your sword seems to be missing."

"Have I still got my boots on?" asked Sir Walter.

"Yes, sir," said Geoffrey.

"Good," said Sir Walter. "Feel down the side of the left-hand one. There should be a tiny pocket-knife in a little pocket down there."

Geoffrey found it. It was a beautiful silver knife in the shape of a fish, with engraved scales and the blade folded back into the body, the edge by which you pulled the blade out forming the dorsal fin.

Geoffrey had some trouble extracting the blade, because of his lack of nails, but he managed it at last and sawed away at the creepers until they were all cut. Sir Walter sat up in the flickering torchlight and took off his helmet.

"Well," he said, easing the back of his neck. "I really thought I was done-for that time. I don't think I could have lasted much longer down there. Come on, let's get out of here before the evil brute comes back."

"He won't come back, sir," said Geoffrey. "He's dead."

"*Dead*?" exclaimed Sir Walter. "But who killed him?"

"*I* did," said Geoffrey proudly.

He could have got away with it. Lancelot was the only witness, and a puppy couldn't tell anyone. Geoffrey could easily have said that *he* had taken the dog and run it round the ogrc's feet, but to his eternal credit he couldn't keep up such a monumental lie for more than two seconds.

"Actually, sir," he said, blushing from head to toe. "It was my puppy who killed him, sir. It was a sort of accident. He got his rope tangled round the ogre's feet, and it fell and hit its head. And the puppy isn't really mine either, sir. I'm sort of looking after him for a friend of mine. Well, it's not *really* a friend sir. Just someone I know."

The sight of Geoffrey blushing almost scarlet made Sir Walter recall the boy he had met on the previous day.

"Haven't I met you before, lad?" he asked, putting his hand under Geoffrey's chin and turning his face towards the light. "Weren't you the boy in the lane yesterday? The one

I had supper with?"

"Yes, sir," mumbled Geoffrey.

"Well, thank heaven you're here now, lad, that's all I can say," said Sir Walter, clambering stiffly to his feet in the battered suit of armour. "We'd better get out of this foul-smelling hole and get some fresh air into our lungs. Now, where's the heroic puppy?"

"He's still tied to the ogre's legs, sir," said Geoffrey. "He's had a dreadful shock, sir. He was so brave, rushing up like that and barking his head off as if the great monster was no more than a mouse, but then it all got a bit much for him, sir. Can I use your knife to cut him free?"

"Of course," replied Sir Walter. "Let's go."

The branch was almost burnt away and Sir Walter held up the remaining twelve inches of wildly flaming wood as they made their way back down the tunnel into the firelit clearing outside.

Chapter Eleven

 ancelot had given up the struggle and was lying still, whimpering softly. Geoffrey hastened to cut the rope, and Lancelot sprang free, leaping up and down with joy, first at Geoffrey, then at Sir Walter. In the end, he was in such a state that he grabbed himself by the tail and proceeded to tear round in circles. Geoffrey and Sir Walter watched, laughing.

"Good gracious me!" exclaimed Sir Walter suddenly. "It's Lancelot, the dog Matilda's been bringing to the office. How on earth

– what's *he* doing here? Come to think of it, what are *you* doing here?"

"It's rather a long story, sir," mumbled Geoffrey nervously, remembering the state of the office, not to mention the stolen cart.

"Then you must tell me," said Sir Walter. "But first, let's get away from here and back to the village. You can explain to me on the way there."

As they picked their way down the hillside by the light of another flaming branch, Geoffrey did his best to explain exactly what had happened. As he talked, Sir Walter nodded and said sympathetic things like "I see", or "That must have been difficult for you." He was *so* sympathetic, in fact, that Geoffrey told him everything, even the bad bits. He told him about wrecking the office and stealing the cart. He even confessed how he had lied to his mother about Sir Walter promising him a job.

Then he asked Sir Walter how he had been caught, and Sir Walter told him how the ogre had been more cunning than ogres usually are and had dug a deep pit near the cave which he and his horse had fallen straight into. The ogre had eaten the horse for tea (Geoffrey noticed that Sir Walter's voice wobbled a bit when he told him that part). Then it had tied Sir Walter with creeper and buried him in the revolting larder. Geoffrey and Lancelot had arrived in the nick of time as the ogre had been building the fire to roast Sir Walter for its dinner.

By this time, the village was in sight. The streets were still completely deserted, but Sir Walter took Geoffrey to the church, where they climbed up to the belfry and rang all the bells over and over, with Lancelot delighted to be allowed to bark to his heart's content.

Doors began to creak open, then a few people carrying lanterns ventured out, and before long there was a huge crowd outside the church. Sir Walter leaned out of the window with Geoffrey in front of him.

"The ogre is dead," he called out. "There is nothing to fear any more. This lad came and saved me with his dog. Remember his name, Geoffrey Strangeways. You will hear great things of him in years to come."

"Oh, I wouldn't say that," muttered Geoffrey modestly.

When they came down from the tower, the villagers hoisted Geoffrey on to their shoulders and carried him round the village green, singing and dancing and calling out "Three cheers for the lad!" and "Well done, Geoffrey the Giant-killer!" and other heartwarming tributes.

Lancelot (who did not mind Geoffrey taking all the credit) pranced about barking and knocking people over.

When everyone had calmed down, the villagers found a horse for Sir Walter and a warm cloak for Geoffrey. Sir Walter climbed into the saddle and swung Geoffrey up in front of him.

"Rowf!" barked Lancelot, looking up in a "Don't forget *me* will you?" sort of way.

"Put the dog up here too," said Sir Walter.

Lancelot was seized by half a dozen villagers, who laid him across the horse's neck with his front paws down one side and his hind paws down the other. At first, he rolled his eyes wildly and tried to get down, but Geoffrey ordered him to stay and held him so tightly that he gave up the fight and decided to be good.

Halfway back to Under-Withy, Geoffrey fell asleep and let go of Lancelot, who promptly fell off. After that, he flatly refused to get on again and ran full-pelt behind them all the way home. Actually, he had enough puppy-energy to run to John O'Groats and back and still be happy to have a quick game of ball.

Chapter Twelve

 t was one o'clock in the morning when they finally arrived at Under-Withy. The front door was locked at home, so Geoffrey flung a handful of pebbles up at the shutters while Lancelot barked helpfully. One of the shutters opened and Geoffrey's mum put her head out clad in a frilly sleeping-bonnet.

"Who is it?" she called nervously into the dark.

"It's us, Mum!" replied Geoffrey, his voice bursting with pride. "Me and Sir Walter, like I told you, and we didn't need the poker after all!"

The travellers were so weary that they collapsed asleep almost at once. Sir Walter slept on Geoffrey's bed and Geoffrey slept on a pile of blankets next to the fire, with Lancelot stretched out against his back like a furry electric blanket.

Mrs Strangeways could not sleep with excitement, planning what she could give her illustrious guest for breakfast. He could have scrambled eggs, or perhaps an egg and mashed potatoes, or a baked potato with an omelette. It was a bit limiting when you only had two eggs and half a sack of potatoes. She would have to sneak down and warn Geoffrey to say he'd have his breakfast later, then Sir Walter could have the two eggs without being embarrassed. She finally fell asleep in the middle of wondering if she could beg a piece of ham off old Mother Redpath next door.

They all got up late. Sir Walter only wanted a cup of tea, insisting that he never had breakfast. Mrs Strangeways didn't know whether to be relieved or disappointed, as she'd decided on fried eggs and chips. She did, however, boil up a kettle and give Sir Walter a basin of hot water and some soap so he could wash the earth and general grime from his face. He had been too exhausted to do any washing the night before.

"Well," said Sir Walter as he finished his second cup of tea, "I think I'll be on my way now!"

Geoffrey's heart suddenly plummeted into his battered old leather boots.

"You'd better take Lancelot with you, sir," he said, pulling the puppy to his feet by the collar. "They'll all be worried sick about him."

"Not when I tell them he's found a new home with you," said Sir Walter. "You *would* like him, wouldn't you?"

"Oh, *yes!*" said Geoffrey, realizing much to his surprise that he had grown completely attached to the animal. "But Matilda's mother – won't she be upset?"

"Quite the opposite," said Sir Walter. "Matilda's mother has become ill with rheumatism and decided she can't keep him. Matilda was only taking him to the office until she found a new home."

"Oh, Lance!" gasped Geoffrey. "You can stay here with *me*, boy!"

The puppy bounced about over-excitedly, picked up the hem of Mrs Strangeways' dress and began to kill it, shaking it from side to side.

"Get *off!*" exclaimed Mrs Strangeways, trying to hold down her skirt and shoo Lancelot away at the same time. "You'll have to train him, Geoffrey, whatever brave deeds he's been doing."

"I will, I will!" said Geoffrey, grabbing Lancelot and shoving him out of the door.

"There's one more thing before I go," said Sir Walter, turning to Geoffrey. "About that job – *you* know, that job I promised you when we met in the lane. Well, I've decided that office-boy isn't quite right for you after all. How would you like to go to knight-school?"

"Knight-school!" breathed Geoffrey. "But – you have to be – well, there aren't actually any peasants at knight-school?"

Sir Walter laughed. "I shall sponsor you, my lad," he continued. "You could start next term, in September. My old school, Axington Armour-Bearers, is an excellent one. Goodness, we had some times there. They've even still got the same wizard in the Spells and Sorcery Department. He must be a hundred and ninety by now; he was positively ancient in *my* day! And you'd be taught jousting and riding and falconry, all that sort of stuff. Well, what do you think?"

"*I* think it sounds marvellous," said Geoffrey. Then a rather dismal thought occurred to him. "The only thing *is*, sir, I've *got* to get some paid work till mother gets better, so we can have something to live on."

"That's settled then," said Sir Walter. "If money's your only worry, I'll pay you to polish up all my armour once a week until your mother is fit again. With a bit of luck, those arms will be healed by September, and even if they aren't you can carry on polishing my armour each week until they *are* better. What do you think, Mrs Strangeways?" he turned politely to Geoffrey's mum, who was looking rather nonplussed in the rocking-chair.

"Oh, I'm sure they *will* be better by then,

sir," she said faintly. "But sir, I was going to send him back to the village school in Greater Rollaround when my arms were better. There's all that uniform to buy for a grand school like the Armour-Bearers, sir. I could *knit* him one, of course, sir, but he might feel a bit, well – *different* next to the other boys."

"My dear Mrs Strangeways," said Sir Walter kindly. "You would not have to pay for anything if I sponsored your boy to go there. I shall take care of it *all*. School fees, uniform, board and lodging. You really would have nothing to worry about."

"Oh, sir," gasped Mrs Strangeways, as this amazing information sank in. "Oh, sir, you really are too kind to us. Say thank you, Geoffrey."

"Thank you, sir," said Geoffrey.

"It's nothing," said Sir Walter. "It's the very least I can do in return for my life. Now then, I really *must* get back to the office and explain to everyone what's been going on. When I've made all the arrangements for the school, I'll send you a letter by carrier-pigeon to the post office at Over-Wallop. You'll have to keep checking to see if it's arrived – probably not till next week."

Geoffrey's mum was so overcome by all the kindness and the thought of her own boy going to such a marvellous school, that she could not think of anything to say, and rocked back and forth in the rocking-chair smiling weakly. Sir Walter solemnly bade her goodbye, even gallantly kissing the fingertips which stuck out of the end of the splints.

Geoffrey went into the front garden to wave goodbye, tripping over Lancelot who was lying outside the front door like a doormat.

He felt suddenly rather shy and shoved his hands into his pockets, where he found Sir Walter's silver fish-shaped knife.

"Oh look, sir," he said, handing it to Sir Walter. "I forgot to give this back to you."

"Keep it," smiled Sir Walter. "And thank you for being there. I would surely have died if you and your dog had not set out to find me so quickly. Come along to the agency next Saturday and Matilda will show you where my armour is kept so that you can polish it all for me. Oh, and don't worry about the office. They won't mind a bit of a mess in exchange for one of their knights.

"Watch out for my letter at the post office. Take care now!" And he swung up on his horse and thundered down the street and away into the countryside.

Geoffrey stood by the gatepost and watched till he was out of sight and the dust had settled in the sharp morning sunlight.

Mrs Strangeways came out into the garden looking rather as if someone had hit her on the head with a cricket bat.

"Isn't it marvellous, Geoffrey?" she said, beaming from ear to ear. "Just think of it! My own son at Axington Armour-Bearers in that nice uniform – learning to ride and do jousting and sorcery and all those clever things. Oooh, I'm so proud of you, going off after that ogre the way you did, cool as a cucumber."

Geoffrey blushed and scuffed his feet along the path.

"Oh, don't make such a fuss, Mother," he mumbled. "It was nothing. Really, it was nothing at all."

THE SUMMERTIME SANTA

It starts with empty boxes... Caireen's match-box is empty and so is her pencil case – which means that Grandad's special pencils are missing. Mum's tennis balls are missing, too. And next door, Edward's box of puzzles has no puzzles in it. It must, the children agree, have something to do with their new neighbours. So off they go to investigate. But what they find is not at all what they are expecting. It's something so sad, so terrible, that it threatens to bring an end to Christmas.

Whether you believe in Santa or not (and it you don't, you'd better watch out), if you like a good story full of humour and surprise, this is the book for you.

"This story is great fun." *Recent Children's Fiction*

HARRY AND CHICKEN

It's not every day you meet a talking cat. And not just a talking cat, but a cat who calls you by your most secret family nickname. That's what happens to Chicken when she meets Harry. But then Harry isn't really a cat at all – he's an extraterrestrial being, stranded on Earth and looking for somewhere to stay. And he's decided to stay with Chicken. The only problem is that Chicken's mother doesn't like cats ... and her sister is allergic to them, and her brother has two budgies, and Harry – well – Harry just can't keep his paws out of trouble!

Harry's unearthly exploits and Chicken's attempts to keep them secret result in all kinds of chaotic fun in this entertaining story for young readers.

THE GLASS BIRD

More than anything else in the world, Adam
wants a friend. One day, walking home from
school Adam picks up a conker and – almost
as a joke – he makes a wish. He wishes for a
friend. But the conker leads him to something
quite different: a glittering bird hidden in the
ferns. It's the most beautiful thing Adam's
ever seen, and the most extraordinary – for the
glass bird appears to live and breathe. Could
it be that this wonderful creature has the
power to make Adam's wish come true?

A magical yet very real story about friendship
and a special secret shared, *The Glass Bird* is
ideal for young readers.

"An enchanting story." *Books for Your Children*

THE WIZARD IN THE WOODS

Ben-Muzzy is a second-class Junior Wizard in the service of the Grand High Wizard, Wollibar. Today, though, he could become a first-class Junior Wizard. All he has to do is get his spells right – and Ben-Muzzy knows his spells backwards. Unfortunately, saying spells backwards can get a wizard into a lot of trouble, especially if it's a vanishing spell. One moment Ben-Muzzy is in the examination room and the next he's ... well! lost in a wood somewhere – which is where the twins, Joel and Gemma, find him. And that's when the real adventures begin.

Wizards, witches, ogres, giants and a pink elephant with blue spots are just a few of the wonders in this funny and magical fantasy, guaranteed to have young readers spellbound.

"Children who enjoy fantasy will find much to entertain them." *The Junior Bookshelf*

MORE WALKER PAPERBACKS
For You to Enjoy